BABAR'S
LITTLE GIRL

BABAR'S
LITTLE GIRL

LAURENT DE BRUNHOFF

Abrams Books for Young Readers
New York

There was big news in Celesteville. Babar and Celeste were expecting another child! They wanted a girl so they would have as many daughters as sons.

One day while out walking, Celeste felt so tired that she had to lie down. "Get the doctor!" she called to Babar. "The baby is coming." Before the doctor got there, the baby was born—a little girl!

She was named Isabelle, and she was an amazing baby. By the time she was only a few months old, she could already stand in her cradle and throw toys.

She had a big appetite and was never tired. At breakfast she was full of energy—unlike her father, who had often been up all night trying to get her to sleep.

As Isabelle grew, her brothers and her sister sometimes got tired of the noise she made.

But sometimes she was very quiet. She loved to watch the insects in the grass.

One day when the children were out for a walk, Isabelle noticed a hippo lying on a turtle.

"Mr. Hippo, would you move, please?" she asked politely. "You're squashing a turtle." But the lazy hippo refused. Isabelle got all the children to push together and roll the hippo away.

"Thank you," said the grateful turtle.

On Isabelle's fifth birthday, Babar and Celeste gave her a big party. All her friends were invited.

The musicians of the Royal Guard played music, and the Old Lady baked a spectacular cake.

Isabelle loved her presents.
    While trying out her new roller skates, she saw a cat in a tree. She coaxed the cat down, took it in her arms, and skated home with it to give it some milk.

She had missed lunch, and Babar was upset. Although it was nice of her to worry about the cat, he said, she had forgotten about her family.

Isabelle felt so bad that she hid behind a bush. She had made everyone worry about her. Her father had scolded her.

Not long after that, the whole family went walking in the mountains. When it was time to head home, Isabelle could not be found.

She had already forgotten the scolding. She was having a lovely time. She walked, she ran, she skipped, and she jumped. She never imagined her family might worry.

She wandered farther and farther until she reached the Blue Valley, home to Boover and Picardee, friends of the family.

"How can I cross the river?" she asked herself. She walked along the shore until she saw an old elephant in a motorboat.

She asked him politely to take her across, and he said he would be happy to.

"You are a polite little girl, and very adventurous."

Isabelle said good-bye to the old elephant. She ran up to the house and knocked at the door.

"Isabelle!" said plump Boover.

"What are you doing here?" said tall Picardee.

"I'm looking for people to play with," she said.

"You've come to the right place!" said Boover and Picardee together.

Isabelle was hungry and thirsty after her trip. They gave her orange juice and cookies.

"Would you like to play hide-and-seek?" asked Boover.

She hid behind the sofa. But Boover found her quickly.

So she ran off, looking for a better place to hide.
The old house was full of surprises.

After the excitement of hide-and-seek, Picardee needed to stand on his head to relax. Isabelle and Boover tried it too. Isabelle was better than Boover. But Boover was good at cards.

They all loved music and were good musicians, so they played some jazz and then danced.

"What a wonderful day!" cried Isabelle.

Tired from all the fun, they turned on the television.

"Our little girl has disappeared," Babar was saying. "Isabelle, if you hear this, please come home immediately."

Isabelle started crying. "I did just what he told me not to do," she said, "and now everyone is worried about me again."

Her two friends were upset too.

"We thought your family knew you were here! We have
to get you home," said Picardee. "What is the fastest way?"

"We must use the hang gliders," said Boover.

From the top of the mountain, they took off on their hang gliders. Isabelle rode on Picardee's back. Her heart raced, but it was such fun!

"We're coming in for a landing!" cried Picardee. "Right at the palace." He touched down nicely. Boover was not so lucky.

Boover and Picardee kissed Isabelle good-bye and went to tell Babar she was safe.

"Come see us again," said Boover.

"But remember to tell your parents first," added Picardee.

Isabelle ran down the stairs to Arthur and Zephir.

Pom, Flora, and Alexander were happy to see her again.

"We missed you," said Alexander.

"Welcome back," said Flora.

"You got to ride on a hang glider," said Pom. "All the exciting things happen to you."

At last Babar and Celeste were reunited with their daughter. They were so grateful to have her home.

"You don't even have to scold me," said Isabelle. "I know I made everyone worry. I am so sorry. Please forgive me."

And of course they did.

The artwork for each picture is prepared using watercolor on paper.
This text is set in 16-point Comic Sans.

The Library of Congress has cataloged the original Abrams edition of this book as follows:

Library of Congress Cataloging-in-Publication Data

Brunhoff, Laurent de.
     Babar's Little Girl / Laurent de Brunhoff.
          p. cm.
     Summary: The arrival of new baby Isabelle creates much excitement in Babar's family,
particularly after she learns to walk and gets lost in the mountains.
     ISBN 0-8109-5703-5
     [1. Elephants—Fiction. 2. Babies—Fiction. 3. Lost children—Fiction.] I. Title.

PZ7.B82843 Babn 2001
[E]—dc21   00-44809

ISBN for this edition: 978-1-4197-0340-9

Printed and bound in China
10 9 8 7 6 5 4 3 2 1

Abrams Books for Young Readers are available at special discounts when purchased in quantity
for premiums and promotions as well as fundraising or educational use. Special editions can also
be created to specification. For details, contact specialsales@abramsbooks.com or the address
below.

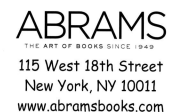

115 West 18th Street
New York, NY 10011
www.abramsbooks.com